Pegasus Princesses
SNOW'S SLIDE

Pegasus Princesses
SNOW'S SLIDE

Emily Bliss

illustrated by **Sydney Hanson**

BLOOMSBURY
CHILDREN'S BOOKS
NEW YORK   LONDON   OXFORD   NEW DELHI   SYDNEY

BLOOMSBURY CHILDREN'S BOOKS
Bloomsbury Publishing Inc., part of Bloomsbury Publishing Plc
1385 Broadway, New York, NY 10018

BLOOMSBURY, BLOOMSBURY CHILDREN'S BOOKS, and the Diana logo
are trademarks of Bloomsbury Publishing Plc

First published in the United States of America in September 2022
by Bloomsbury Children's Books
www.bloomsbury.com

Bloomsbury books may be purchased for business or promotional use. For information on
bulk purchases please contact Macmillan Corporate and Premium Sales Department at
specialmarkets@macmillan.com

Library of Congress Cataloging-in-Publication Data
available upon request
ISBN 978-1-5476-0972-7 (paperback) • ISBN 978-1-5476-0973-4 (e-book)

Book design by John Candell
Typeset by Westchester Publishing Services
Printed and bound in the U.S.A.
2 4 6 8 10 9 7 5 3 1 (paperback)

All papers used by Bloomsbury Publishing, Inc., are natural, recyclable products
made from wood grown in well-managed forests. The manufacturing processes
conform to the environmental regulations of the country of origin.

To find out more about our authors and books visit www.bloomsbury.com
and sign up for our newsletters.

For Phoenix and Lynx

Pegasus Princesses
SNOW'S SLIDE

Chapter One

"What should we name it?" Clara Griffin asked her younger sister, Miranda.

The two girls—wearing matching light blue snowsuits and green winter boots—stood side by side on a white sheet spread over their living room carpet. Together, they admired the snow-covered mountain they had built by draping five white sheets over an enormous mound of cushions, pillows, coats, stuffed animals, sleeping bags, beanbag chairs, towels, and balled-up blankets.

"Mount Snow?" Miranda suggested. She frowned. "That's too boring. Can you think of a more creative name?"

"Hmm," Clara said. "Mount Mongolopticus?"

Miranda laughed. "Mount Mongolopticus," she repeated. "That's perfect. Do you think the snow leopards are ready to go mitten-sliding?"

Clara turned to the coffee table, which she and her sister had pushed into a corner to make space for their mountain. On the table's glass top lay four snow leopards

the sisters had made out of twigs, string, dandelion fluff, and glue. The leopards were napping while their glue dried. "I bet they're ready now," Clara said. "Should I go get them?"

Miranda paused. She let out a long sigh. "The only problem is I'm really, really hot in my snowsuit."

Clara nodded. She had to admit she was also feeling too hot. After all, it was a sunny, warm spring day. "Let's take them off for a little while," Clara said.

Miranda scrunched up her nose. "We can't play Snowy Mountain without wearing snowsuits."

"What if we just pretend to wear them?" Clara suggested.

"It's not the same," Miranda said, shaking her head.

Clara sighed. Miranda was right that wearing a snowsuit and pretending to wear a snowsuit weren't exactly the same. But Clara noticed drops of sweat forming on her forehead, and her shirt felt damp against her back. The sisters needed to cool off somehow. And then Clara had an idea. She hopped from one foot to the other. "I know what we can do!" she exclaimed. "I'll be right back!"

Clara raced into the kitchen, leaped across the tile floor to the refrigerator, and opened the freezer door. On one of the shelves was a clear plastic bin full of reusable ice packs that she and her sister put in their school lunches to keep them cool. Clara grabbed the entire bin, swung the freezer door shut, and rushed back to the living room. She placed the bin on the floor between her and her sister.

"What are those for?" Miranda asked, raising her eyebrows.

"Watch this!" Clara said. She unzipped the top of her snowsuit. Then she picked up an ice pack and dropped it right inside her suit. The ice pack settled next to her left knee. She picked up two more ice packs and dropped them into the back of her suit. Her damp shirt instantly felt cool.

Miranda giggled. She unzipped her snowsuit and dropped one ice pack into the front and one into the back. Her eyes widened and she grinned. "Good idea, Clara," she said. "I'm starting to feel cooler already."

Clara and Miranda giggled as they dropped ice pack after ice pack into their snowsuits. When the bin was empty, they both zipped themselves back up.

"Let's roll on the floor to move the ice packs around," Clara said. She flopped down and rolled across the white sheet, enjoying the feeling of the ice packs shifting across her stomach, legs, and back.

Miranda crouched down and did two somersaults. She did a cartwheel. And then she rolled over to Clara. "Now I'm the perfect temperature," she said.

"Me too!" Clara said. "Are you ready for leopard mitten-sliding now?"

Miranda nodded. "I'll go wake up the snow leopards while you get the mittens," she suggested.

"Perfect," Clara said. She stood up and skipped to the front hall closet to get the wicker basket her family used to store mittens. But the shelf where it belonged was bare. And then she remembered: Two days before, she had used the basket as a tent for her plastic penguin figures and the mittens as their nests. Clara raced back through the living room, up the stairs, down the hall, and into her bedroom.

Clara stepped over a climbing dome she had built for her popsicle-stick pegasus figures out of metal forks and masking tape. She sidled around pictures of polar bears and arctic foxes she had made by gluing white azalea petals onto black construction paper. She smiled at her puppy, Quack, who was fast asleep in a pile of clean laundry on the floor. And then she walked along a winding trail of wooden train track pieces, books, dominoes, animal flash cards, and ceramic coasters. At the end of the trail was the penguin tent she had made by turning the mitten basket upside down, so its handle propped it partway up. On the floor, under the basket, was a row of knit mittens, each with a small penguin nestled inside it. Clara gently pulled the penguins out of their nests and arranged them around a campfire she made from a crumpled red sock. Then she grabbed the mittens and ran toward her bedroom door.

As Clara stepped out into the hallway, she heard a high-pitched humming noise. At first she thought it might be a leaf blower outside or even music playing in her parents' bedroom. But as the humming grew louder, Clara realized the sound was coming from under her bed.

Clara grinned from ear to ear. She turned around and rushed over to her bed, kneeled, and pulled out a flip-top shoebox she had decorated with glitter, paint, and markers. She opened the box to reveal a large silver feather. Light shot up and down the feather's spine as it hummed louder and louder. The feather had been a gift from the pegasus princesses—eight royal pegasus sisters who ruled over the Wing Realm, a magical world in which all the creatures had wings. Whenever the pegasus princesses wanted to invite Clara to visit them, the feather shimmered and hummed— just the way it was shimmering and humming right then. To get to the Wing Realm, all Clara had to do was hold the feather in her hand as she ran to a special clearing in the woods surrounding her house.

Clara couldn't wait to see her pegasus friends. Each one had a unique magic power: silver Princess Mist could turn invisible; teal Princess Aqua could breathe underwater and make bubbles; peach Princess Flip could do a somersault and turn into any animal; black Princess Star had extraordinary senses; pink Princess Rosie could speak and understand any language; white Princess Snow could freeze things and create winter weather; green Princess Stitch could sew, knit, or crochet almost anything; and purple Princess Dash could instantly transport herself anywhere in the Wing Realm.

Clara picked up the feather. It immediately stopped humming. Holding both the bunch of mittens and the feather, Clara ran back across her room. When she got to the door, she paused and looked down. She knew that she should probably take off her snowsuit and snow boots before visiting the Wing Realm. But it always felt like taking off her winter gear took forever, and she didn't want to wait any longer to visit the pegasus princesses. And besides, she loved the feeling of the ice packs inside her snowsuit. Clara decided that if she wanted to, she could always take her suit off at Feather Palace, the pegasus princesses' wing-shaped home.

Clara slid the feather into her snowsuit

pocket. She ran along the hall, down the stairs, and into the living room. She handed her sister the mittens. "I'm going to go outside to get some pine needles to make beds for the snow leopards after they finish sledding," Clara said. "I'll be right back." Time in the human world froze while Clara was in the Wing Realm, meaning that even if she spent hours with her pegasus friends, Miranda would think she had been gone for only a few minutes.

"Can I go ahead and put the snow leopards inside the mittens?" Miranda asked.

"Definitely," Clara said. "You can even start letting them slide down Mount Mongolopticus."

"Okay," Miranda said, and she smiled as she gently pushed a snow leopard into a red wool mitten.

Clara skipped across the living room, through the kitchen, and out the back door. She hopped in her boots along the slate walkway that led across her yard and into the woods. She pulled the feather out of her pocket as she splashed through the creek where she and her sister liked to play potions. She ran down a hill, turned a corner, and entered a clearing by a large pine tree.

Glittery light swirled and flashed. A green armchair with silver wings on its back appeared. "Hello, chair!" Clara sang out. She slipped the feather back into her pocket.

The chair hopped excitedly. It jumped into the air and did a somersault. And then it slid across the carpet of pine needles to Clara.

She smiled and patted the chair's back before she turned and sat down. She gripped the chair's arms as the chair soared up into the air and landed on top of the large pine tree. The trunk swayed for a moment, and then the chair leaped forward. It slid across the green tile roof of Clara's house, bounced off the top of the chimney, and launched straight up into the sky. As the chair climbed higher and higher, it began to spin faster and faster. Then everything went pitch black until, a few seconds later, the chair landed with a loud clatter.

Chapter Two

Clara looked all around her. She knew exactly where she was: the front hall of Feather Palace. On the magenta walls hung portraits of the pegasus princesses and their silver pet cat, Lucinda. Rainbow water spouted from marble pegasus-shaped fountains. Pegasus sculptures, with feathered wings outstretched, reared up from pedestals. Light from the chandeliers danced on the black tile floors. In the center of the room were the pegasus princesses' eight thrones, arranged in a half circle. Next to Snow's white throne was Lucinda's sofa—a cat-size silver couch with a back shaped like a cat head and two green sequin eyes. On the cat sofa's cushion was a small star-shaped pillow that Clara had given to Lucinda for her birthday.

Clara turned to her right and blinked her eyes in surprise. On the tile floor, next to the thrones, was a giant frozen puddle. All eight pegasus princesses huddled in a tight circle by the far edge of the ice. Just above them, Lucinda fluttered her wings as she hovered upside down in the air.

Snow flicked her white mane, swished her white tail, and said, "I'll show you how to do it one more time. Then we can all practice for a few more minutes."

The seven other pegasus princesses lined up along either side of the ice and stared intently at Snow.

Snow trotted to the wall farthest from the ice. She turned toward the frozen puddle and stared at it for a few seconds. Then she took a deep breath, furrowed her brow, and galloped toward the ice at top speed. When she had almost reached it, she extended her wings for balance and jumped forward. With a joyful whinny, she landed on her belly with her legs splayed out on either side of her. She grinned with delight as she slid the length of the frozen puddle.

When she reached the end of ice, she stood up on the tile floor and smiled encouragingly at her sisters. "That's all you'll have to do," she explained. "It might be a little harder this afternoon because you'll be going down a slide instead of across a frozen puddle. But I know you'll all be able to do it as long as we practice now."

Mist, Aqua, Flip, Star, Rosie, Stitch, and Dash reared up with excitement. All eight pegasus princesses trotted to the far wall. They turned to face the frozen puddle. And then, all at once, they galloped toward the ice. They extended their wings, jumped forward, and slid on their bellies across the frozen puddle. Clara noticed that Mist, Aqua, Flip, Star, Rosie, Snow, and Stitch whinnied and laughed as they slid. But Dash snorted and frowned. When they got to the end of the ice, Mist, Aqua, Flip, Star,

Rosie, Snow, and Stitch called out, "That was incredible!" and, "Let's do it again!" and, "We should install an ice rink in the basement of the palace!" They stood up on the tiles, reared up, and galloped back to the far wall to slide again. They didn't notice Dash clambering slowly onto the tile floor and, with her head down and her tail between her legs, trotting over to her purple throne.

As Mist, Aqua, Flip, Star, Rosie, Snow, and Stitch kept sliding across the ice, Dash curled up on her throne, hung her head, and blinked away tears. Clara stood up and walked over to Dash.

"Are you okay?" Clara asked. She gently put her hand on Dash's back.

Dash looked up in surprise. When she saw Clara, she smiled as tears streamed down her cheeks. "Clara!" she said. "I'm happy you're here." She sighed and shook her head. "And I also feel sad and disappointed. I was so excited about going ice-sliding this afternoon with my sisters. But just now, when I practiced on real ice for the first time, I realized I absolutely hate the feeling of the ice. It's cold and slippery and horrible. Now I'm going to have a terrible afternoon!"

Clara nodded. She could understand what it felt like to really want to do something, only to discover she didn't like it after all. The previous year, she had spent months wanting to take a ballet class.

When her parents finally signed her up for one, she discovered that she hated the feeling of her tights and leotard against her skin, that the music in the ballet studio felt too loud for her ears, and that she enjoyed making up her own dance moves much more than she liked learning ballet steps. She had felt sad, disappointed, and angry—just the way Dash seemed to feel right then. "I can really relate to how you feel," Clara said. She wrapped her arms around Dash and gave her a hug. "I felt exactly the same way about ballet. I really wanted to do it. And then when I tried it, I hated it."

"Ballet?" Dash said. "What is *that*?"

Clara laughed. "It's just a kind of dance

in the human world," she said. It was refreshing to talk to someone who hadn't even heard of ballet. "A few of my friends really love it. But I do not. In fact, I can't stand it!"

Dash nodded. "Well, that's exactly how I feel about ice." She paused, and her face brightened. "But I feel a little better already because you're here." Dash turned toward her sisters, who were whinnying as they slid on their bellies across the ice. "Guess what!" Dash called out. "Clara's here!"

Mist, Aqua, Flip, Star, Rosie, Snow, and Stitch looked at Clara. They whinnied even louder. And then they scrambled off the ice and galloped over to her. Lucinda purred loudly as she flew across the front hall and swooped down to her cat sofa.

"My human girl is back!" Mist called out.

"Welcome to Feather Palace," Aqua said, trotting in a circle around Clara.

"We're so glad you've joined us," Flip said.

"You're arrived in time for the best afternoon ever," Star said.

"You're going to love what we have planned," Rosie said.

"Snow will tell you all about it," Stitch said.

"You've gotten here just in time," Snow

gushed, flicking her mane and swishing her tail. "Today is a very special day. We're all going ice-sliding in the Sky Tundra for the first time. We've invited our good friends the snow leopard princesses from the Snow Realm to join us. And we're really hoping you'll come too. Will you? Please?"

"Absolutely!" Clara said. Ice-sliding with snow leopard princesses and pegasus princesses sounded like an amazing way to spend the afternoon.

"Fantastic!" Snow said. Then Snow looked at Clara, furrowed her brow, and cocked her head to the side. That's when Clara noticed that Lucinda and all eight pegasus princesses were staring at her snowsuit and boots.

"Um," Stitch said. "I don't mean to be rude, but . . ."

"I'm just wondering . . ." Mist began.

"I don't know quite how to ask this, but . . ." Flip faltered.

Snow giggled nervously and said, "What we're all wondering is what in the world is that thing you're wearing on your body?"

"And what are those weird, clunky things on your feet?" Aqua said.

Clara laughed. "This is called a snow-suit," she said, touching the fabric of her suit. "And these," she said, lifting up one foot and then the other, "are called snow boots. Humans wear snowsuits and boots in the winter to stay warm."

"Interesting," Snow said, furrowing her brow even more. "How do they work?"

"Well," Clara said, thinking about it for a moment, "they're made of a special material that holds my body heat in and keeps the cold out."

The pegasus princesses nodded thoughtfully. "I've never seen anything like that," Stitch said.

"Is it winter in Gardenview, New Jersey?" Snow asked. Gardenview, New Jersey, was the name of the place where Clara and her family lived.

Clara shook her head. "Actually, it's late spring," she said. "My sister and I were playing a game we made up called Snowy Mountain. That's why we put on our winter gear."

"It's a good thing you're wearing your snowsuit and boots," Snow said. "The ice slide is in the Sky Tundra. And it's pretty cold up there."

Just then, Snow noticed Dash's sad, disappointed face.

"What's wrong?" Snow asked.

Dash sighed and snorted. "I've discovered that I hate the feeling of the ice," she said. "It's too cold and too slippery. I was excited to go ice-sliding this afternoon. But now I'll have to just watch. And I hate just watching while everyone else has fun."

Mist, Aqua, Flip, Star, Rosie, Stitch, and Snow frowned.

"Maybe you'll get used to the feeling of the ice if you practice sliding a few more times," Aqua said hopefully. "Sometimes I don't like the way water feels when I first start swimming. But after a few minutes, it doesn't bother me at all."

Dash shook her head. "Thank you for your suggestion, but I don't think so. I hated the feeling of the ice so much I don't ever want to touch it again."

"Maybe the ice on the ice slide will be less cold and slippery," Snow said.

"Maybe," Dash said. "But probably not. I have a bad feeling all ice feels about the same."

Snow nodded. "You're right," she said. "All the ice I've ever felt—and I've felt a lot of ice—has been cold and slippery." She sighed and smiled apologetically at Dash. "I hate to leave while you're feeling upset, but it's about time for Clara and me to go to the Sky Tundra to greet the snow leopard princesses and decorate the ice slide with balloons."

"While Snow and I are flying to the Sky Tundra, I'll start trying to think of a creative way you can still participate," Clara said to Dash.

"Really?" Dash asked.

"Really," Clara said with a wink.

Snow kneeled so Clara could climb onto her back. But right then, Lucinda flew right up to Clara's face. She touched her pink cat nose to the tip of Clara's nose. "Before you

leave for the Sky Tundra," she purred. "Can we please, please, please play one guessing game?"

Clara giggled and looked at Snow. "Is there time to play one guessing game before we go?" she asked.

Snow smiled. "There's time for one game as long as Lucinda only gets three guesses. Yesterday, I gave Lucinda fifty tries to guess my favorite month, and our guessing game lasted thirty minutes."

"Aren't there only twelve months to choose from?" Clara asked.

"I guessed a lot of imaginary months. Like Octarchuary. And Novembrilune. And Septgustuly. But I forgot January," Lucinda sniffed. She twitched her tail, flew in a circle around Clara's head, and landed on Clara's shoulder. "How about if I guess what the shirt under your snowsuit looks like in three guesses?" she asked. "That should be easy-peasy-lemon-squeezy."

"Okay," Clara said. She tried to remember what shirt she was wearing. She couldn't even recall getting dressed that morning. That meant she was probably still wearing her pajamas.

"I know!" Lucinda said. "Does your shirt have a picture of a winged silver cat on it?"

"I wish it did," Clara said, thinking she would love to own that shirt. "But that's not it."

"Rats!" Lucinda said. She leaped up into the air, turned upside down, and said, "I'll get it this time. Does it have a picture of my cat sofa on it?"

Clara shook her head. "I'm afraid not," she said. She had to admit that she didn't particularly want a shirt with a picture of piece of furniture on the front.

"Double rats!" Lucinda said. She swooped down and landed right on Clara's snow boots. "Does it have a picture of my silver cat dish on it?" she guessed.

Clara shook her head again. "It turns out I'm wearing a pajama top covered in purple penguins," she said. She unzipped her snowsuit a few inches to show Lucinda.

"Triple rats!" Lucinda said. In a huff, she marched toward her cat sofa, waving her tail in the air. That's when Clara noticed that the tip of Lucinda's tail was covered in something black.

"What's on your tail?" Clara asked.

"Just black ink from addressing the

ice-sliding invitation to the snow leopard princesses," Lucinda said, jumping onto her sofa. "I painted the words with my tail."

"I bet you'll win our next guessing game," Clara said in a kind voice as Lucinda began to lick the fur on her leg.

Clara zipped back up her snowsuit as Snow kneeled again in front of her.

Clara swung her leg over Snow's back and sat between her wings. Snow turned to her sisters. "I'll see all of you at the Ice Slide in about an hour."

"I'll come early to help you get ready," Stitch said.

"See you soon!" Mist, Aqua, and Flip called out.

Star and Rosie swished their tails excitedly.

Dash smiled, but her eyes looked sad and anxious.

With Clara on her back, Snow jumped over the frozen puddle and galloped straight for the palace's double doors. The doors magically swung open, and Snow leaped out into the sky. For a few seconds, Clara turned around and admired Feather Palace. The silver, wing-shaped castle sparkled in the sun as it hovered above an ocean of green treetops.

Chapter Three

Snow soared higher and higher into the clear blue sky. "I absolutely cannot wait to show you the Sky Tundra and the ice slide," she said. "And I'm thrilled to introduce you to the snow leopard princesses. This is going to be the best afternoon ever."

"I can't wait, either," Clara said.

"Lucinda really wanted to make and send the invitation to the snow leopard princesses," Snow said. "She only recently learned to paint letters with her tail. And sometimes she still gets letters mixed up. But I let her make the invitation anyway."

Clara smiled as she imagined Lucinda painting letters with her tail.

Snow was silent for a few seconds. And then she said, "I feel so bad for Dash. She's been just as excited as me to go ice-sliding."

"Me too," Clara said. "I can definitely understand how disappointed she feels."

"I have to admit that I don't understand what bothers her so much about the ice,"

Snow said. "To me the ice feels exciting and refreshing. How could she not like it?"

"Everyone feels things differently," Clara said. "The way the ice feels to you or me might be completely different than how it feels to her."

"Huh," Snow said. "I hadn't really thought about it that way."

"I'm hoping we can think of a way for Dash to go ice-sliding without having to feel the ice," Clara said.

"What would you call ice-sliding without feeling the ice? Not-ice-sliding?" Snow asked playfully.

Clara giggled. "How about nice-sliding," she suggested.

"Nice-sliding," Snow repeated. "I like that name!" She nodded toward a glittery white cloud in the distance. "That's the entrance to the Sky Tundra."

Snow beat her wings faster, soared in a circle above the cloud, and landed on it. As soon as her hooves touched the cloud's surface, she slid forward. The cloud was covered in a layer of smooth, flat ice! A wall made of ice bricks lined the edges of the cloud. Built into the wall was an archway made of giant silver snowflakes.

Snow spun and twirled on her shiny white hooves. She kneeled and Clara climbed off her back. Clara slowly slid one of her boots forward and then the other. She had expected to feel like she might lose

her balance and fall over. But instead she felt as though she were ice skating. "Try spinning," Snow said, doing another turn on her hooves. Clara sucked in her breath and spun around in her boots. "Whee!" Clara said. She and Snow glided in circles together around the cloud, twirling, jumping, and spinning in the air.

After a few minutes, Snow winked at Clara and said, "Follow me." Snow slid on her hooves toward the snowflake archway. As soon as she glided under it, she disappeared.

Clara took a deep breath and slid on her boots over to the archway. She bent her knees and did a spinning jump through it.

A second later, Clara landed in a vast, snow-covered field next to Snow. A few feet in front of them was another snowflake archway just like the one on the cloud. Clara noticed other archways dotting the field in the distance.

"Welcome to the Sky Tundra," Snow said with a grin. "I was just thinking we have time for a little bit of fun before we need to blow up balloons and greet the snow leopard princesses," she said. "Is there any chance you'd like to visit the Penguin Artist Colony on our way to the Ice Slide?"

Clara's eyes widened. "That sounds amazing," she said. She wasn't entirely sure what a Penguin Artist Colony was, but she knew she liked art and she knew she liked penguins.

"Fantastic," Snow said. "These magic archways are all over the Sky Tundra. I installed them because even though the penguins have wings, they can't fly. They needed a way to get around the Sky Tundra that's quicker than waddling. I'll show you how they work. Come stand with me under this one."

Clara and Snow stepped forward under the archway. In a flash of glittery light, two red sleds appeared side by side. "Climb on," Snow said with a smile. She stepped onto one of the sleds. Clara stepped onto the other. They both sat down. "Please take us to the Penguin Artist Colony," Snow said.

Immediately, the sleds bolted forward in the snow. "Whee!" Clara said, laughing as they picked up speed. The sleds raced across the snowy field, down a hill, through an icy tunnel, across another snowy meadow, and then stopped under another archway. A few feet in front of them was a tall wall made of ice bricks with a penguin-shaped purple door. Above the door was a sign made of grape-colored gemstones that read, "Penguin Artist Colony."

Snow and Clara stood up and stepped off of the sleds and into the snow. It came up to Clara's knees! In a flash of light, the

sleds disappeared. Snow led the way to the penguin-shaped door and used her nose to push a beak-shaped lavender doorbell. There was a high-pitched chiming noise. After a few seconds, the door swung open. Three plum-colored penguins with long beaks, thin wings, and bright violet eyes waddled out. One penguin wore a beret, another wore a scarf, and another wore a smock spattered with paint.

"Princess Snow!" all three said excitedly.

"Hello!" Snow said. "Priscilla, Penelope, and Petra, this is my dear human friend, Clara. Clara, this is Priscilla," Snow said, nodding to the penguin wearing a beret. "This is Petra." Snow nodded at the one wearing a scarf. "And this is Penelope," she finished, nodding at the one wearing a smock.

"Welcome to our artist colony," Priscilla said.

"Sorry I'm a little messy," Penelope said, looking down at her smock. "I was just painting one of our sculptures."

"Come on in," Petra said. "We'd be thrilled to give you a tour."

Clara and Snow followed the penguins through the door. Immediately in front of them was a row of three lavender-and-white tents.

"Princess Stitch made these tents for us because we were getting too cold at night," Petra said. "Want to see inside them?"

"Absolutely," Snow said.

"I'd love to," Clara said.

Priscilla, Penelope, and Petra waddled forward to the middle tent. "Let's go in this one," Petra said. "This morning we accidentally ripped a giant hole in the one to our left," she continued.

"Now we have a rule," Penelope said. "If we jump in the tents, we have to point our beaks downward."

Petra, Priscilla, and Penelope all looked down so their beaks were tucked against their chests. And then they started jumping. "Like this," Priscilla explained.

"Yes," Petra said. "Just like this. I even wrote a poem to help us remember the rule: 'If you jump around, put your beak down!'"

Clara giggled. "That's a great poem," she said. She glanced to her left. Sure enough, the tent on the end had a giant rip across its ceiling.

The penguins stopped jumping and untucked their beaks. "We're hoping that if we give Princess Stitch a sculpture, she'll be generous enough to make us a new tent," Petra said.

"I have a feeling she'll be happy to help you," Snow said with a wink. "Stitch loves sewing projects. Maybe she can even find some beak-proof fabric."

"The other two tents still work perfectly," Petra said, using her beak to unzip a flap in the middle tent. "They're made of a special magic material Stitch found in the Fabric Forest. It holds in heat. Come right this way."

Clara and Snow followed the three penguins through the open tent flap. Then Penelope used her beak to zip the tent closed again.

Inside was a circle of penguin-sized nests made of lavender fuzz. In the middle of the nests was a small bonfire with rainbow flames. The tent was so much warmer inside that Clara immediately unzipped her snowsuit. She was also glad the ice packs inside her suit were still frozen.

"We love to sleep in here," Petra said.

"I don't mind making art in icy conditions," Penelope said.

"But after a long day sculpting and painting in the cold, it's amazing to have a warm place to go," Priscilla said.

"Your tent is incredible," Clara said. "But I have to admit, I'm getting a little too hot."

"That's probably because of your . . . what was it called?" Snow said. "A slowsnoot?"

Clara laughed. "A snowsuit," she said.

"Oh right," Snow said. "Come to think of it, it sounds like a costume to look like me!" Snow turned to the penguins. "Would you be up for letting us look at the ice sculptures now?"

"Our pleasure!" Petra said. She waddled to a flap on the tent wall opposite where they had entered. She unzipped it, and Clara and Snow followed the penguins out into a snowy field full of purple penguins working on ice sculptures. Four penguins used their beaks to chisel spirals onto the horn of a unicorn sculpture. Another penguin used her wings to shape the mane on a griffin sculpture. Two penguins held paintbrushes in their mouths as they painted a phoenix sculpture bright red. Five penguins pecked tufts of fur onto the ears of a sculpture of a mother lynx with her babies. Clara also noticed sculptures of trees, fairies, mushrooms, foxes, sunflowers, and giant acorns.

"I love your sculptures," Clara said.

"Thank you," Petra said.

"How do you decide what to make?" Clara asked.

"It just comes to us all of a sudden," Priscilla explained.

And then Petra's eyes widened. The

edges of her beak curled upward in an excited smile. "I feel an idea coming on," she said.

Priscilla looked at Petra. Her eyes widened. "Oooh. I do too!" she said.

"Yes!" Penelope said. "The idea is almost here."

The three penguins stared at each other. Then, all at once, they raised up their wings, pointed their beaks toward the sky, and exclaimed in unison, "I feel inspired!"

Glittery white light flashed and swirled. And then a large block of ice, just a little taller than Clara, appeared in front of the penguins. They immediately began using their beaks to chisel and chip off chunks of ice. With their wings, they sliced, shaped, and smoothed the ice. After a minute, Clara could see that the penguins were sculpting a girl—a smiling girl with wavy hair wearing a puffy snowsuit and clunky snow boots. It was Clara! When they finished, the penguins stepped back and admired their work. "What do you think?" Petra asked.

"Do you like it?" Penelope asked.

Priscilla looked at her expectantly.

"I love it," Clara said. "No one has ever made a sculpture of me before. Thank you so much!"

Petra smiled proudly.

"When artistic inspiration hits, you have to follow it," Priscilla said.

Penelope nodded.

"I have another idea!" Petra said. She waddled to the phoenix sculpture and picked up a set of paints and paintbrush with her wings. She waddled back to Clara and handed them to her. "Want to paint your sculpture?" she asked.

Clara jumped up and down with excitement. "Yes!" she exclaimed. She looked at the sculpture and then at the rainbow of paint colors. She decided it was much too boring to paint the sculpture the same colors she was. She dipped the brush in the green paint. And then she painted the skin on her hands and face bright green. She wiped the brush off in the snow and painted her hair pink. Next she painted her eyes yellow, her lips orange, her snowsuit red, and her boots purple.

She stepped back and looked at the colorful version of herself. "What do you think?" she asked.

"I love it," Priscilla said.

"Perfect color choices," Petra said.

"I love your vision," Penelope said.

"Thank you," Clara said.

"I am sorry to end this artistic fun," Snow said, "but I think Clara and I had better head to the ice slide. The snow leopard princesses will be there soon, and we need to welcome them. We also need to blow up some balloons."

"Thank you so much for visiting us," Petra said.

"Please come back any time," Penelope said.

"And thank you for being our special guest artist," Priscilla said.

"It was wonderful to meet you," Clara said. "Thank you so much for showing me your tents and sculptures."

Snow and Clara walked back through the sculptures and around the row of tents. They walked out the penguin door and up to the snowflake archway. Two red sleds appeared, and Snow and Clara climbed into them. "Please take us to the ice slide," Snow said.

The sleds slid across the snowy field. They glided around a hill, through two more tunnels made of ice, down a steep mountain, and around a sharp right turn. They pulled up to another snowflake archway. Just beyond it was a box of purple balloons and a massive puddle of water. Lounging in the puddle were four glowing, bright red leopards.

Chapter Four

Snow and Clara climbed out of their sleds. For several seconds, Snow stared at the puddle and the red leopards with her mouth open and her eyes wide. Finally, she whispered, "Oh no."

"What's wrong?" Clara asked. "Where is the ice slide?" She was suddenly too warm again, and she unzipped the front of her snowsuit.

Snow's Slide

Snow took a long deep breath and nodded toward the puddle. "This is where the ice slide was. But now it's gone."

"Are those the snow leopards?" Clara asked.

Snow shook her head. "The snow

leopards are fluffy and white. I've never seen those leopards before in my life." Snow's bottom lip quivered and her eyes filled with tears.

Clara wrapped her arms around Snow and gave her a hug. "I'm going to go find out who those leopards are and see if they can tell me what happened," she said.

Clara waded through the giant puddle toward the red leopards. Even though her boots were too hot, she was glad she was wearing them as she tromped through the water. When she was a few feet away from the leopards, she smiled. "Hello," she said. "My name is Clara."

The leopards stood up with a splash and grinned excitedly.

"I'm Gladys," one said.

"I'm Glenda," another said.

"I'm Gilbert," another said.

"And I'm Gordon," the last one said.

"We're here for ice-sliding," Gladys explained. The other three leopards nodded eagerly.

"It's wonderful to meet you," Clara said. "Would you mind telling me what kind of animal you are?" She wiped some sweat from her forehead. It was even warmer up close to the leopards.

Gladys grinned. "We're glow leopards," she said.

"From the Glow Realm," Glenda added.

"We got an invitation to come here to go ice-sliding," Gladys explained.

"It was exciting because no one ever invites us to do anything," Gordon said.

"Everyone always complains it's too hot to be near us," Gilbert said, frowning sadly.

"And everyone complains that we melt things," Glenda added.

"We've only ever been invited to an ice cream party once," Gladys said.

"It was a disaster," Gordon admitted. "It turns out no one really wants mint chocolate chip *soup* for dessert."

All four leopards nodded with a forlorn look on their faces.

"It means the world to us to be invited here," Gladys said.

"We were so excited, we got here really, really early," Gordon said.

"We've been waiting for hours," Glenda explained, nodding.

"We're so glad you're here," Clara said, wanting to make sure the glow leopards felt welcome. "But, just out of curiosity, was this giant puddle here when you arrived?"

The glow leopards shook their heads. "When we got here, there was a huge slide made out of ice," Gilbert said.

"I have a feeling we accidentally melted it," Glenda said.

"Sorry about that!" all four glow leopards said.

"Don't worry," Clara said. "I'm sure we

can find a way to still go ice-sliding. If you'll excuse me for just a moment, I need to go talk to Princess Snow. She's that white pegasus over there," Clara added, pointing.

The glow leopards looked at Snow and grinned. Gladys called out, "Hello, Princess Snow! Thanks for inviting us!"

From the edge of the giant puddle, Snow smiled uncertainly. She called back, "Hello, um, leopards!"

Clara fanned herself and wiped sweat from her forehead. And then she waded back through the water to Snow.

"What did you find out?" Snow asked in a worried whisper. "Who in the world are those leopards?"

"Their names are Gladys, Glenda,

Gilbert, and Gordon. They're glow leopards from the Glow Realm," Clara said.
"They say they received an invitation to go
ice-sliding. They also apologized for accidentally melting the slide."

"*Glow* leopards from the *Glow* Realm?"
Snow repeated, looking confused. And
then a flash of understanding came over
her face. "Do you think Lucinda accidentally painted the word 'glow' instead of
'snow' on the invitation?"

Clara nodded. "I bet that's what
happened."

"What a disaster," Snow said, shaking
her head. Her eyes filled with tears.
"We have no choice but to cancel ice-sliding
and send the glow leopards home. Even if

we could think of a way to quickly rebuild the ice slide, the glow leopards would melt it again."

"The thing is," Clara said, "the glow leopards are thrilled to be here. They told me they never get invited to do anything because everyone else complains they're too hot to be around."

"Oh dear," Snow said. "In that case, I would feel terrible just sending them home."

Just then, Stitch pulled up to the arch-way on a sled. She looked at the puddle and the glow leopards, then galloped over to Snow and Clara. "What in the world happened?" she asked. "And who are those leopards?"

Clara and Snow explained everything they had learned to Stitch.

"Oh no," Stitch said. "Should I fly back and tell the others not to come? Or should we change our plan to some kind of swim-ming party?"

Clara took a long, deep breath. "Before we cancel or change anything, let's first take a moment and see if we can think of a creative solution that will let us rebuild the slide *and* include the glow leopards," she said.

"I'll do absolutely anything to help," Snow said.

"Me too," Stitch said.

Snow furrowed her brow and stared

down at her hooves. Stitch sucked in her lips and closed her eyes. Clara took another deep breath. She looked at the box of balloons and then at the puddle. She thought about the penguins' tents and sculptures. She glanced at Snow's snowflake tiara and Stitch's scissors, needle, and thread tiara. And then, suddenly, Clara had an idea. She grinned and jumped up and down.

Snow looked up at Clara. "Have you actually thought of a plan to go ice-sliding with the glow leopards?" she asked, looking both hopeful and disbelieving.

Stitch opened her eyes in surprise.

"I think I have an idea," Clara said. "The first thing we need to do is ask the penguins if we can use their torn tent for a sewing project."

"I'll go ask," Stitch said. "I'll fly there instead of riding the magic sleds since that's faster."

"Thank you," Clara said. "And could you also ask the penguins if they might be willing to come help us?"

"Sure thing," Stitch said. She beat her wings and soared up into the air toward the Penguin Artist Colony.

While they waited for Stitch to return with the ripped tent and the penguins, Clara picked up the box of balloons and carried it to the edge of the puddle. She kneeled next to the box, grabbed a balloon, and held it under the puddle. She stretched the opening with her fingers to fill the balloon up with water. Then she tied the end and filled up another balloon, and then another. When she had filled up all the balloons, she returned them to the box.

Just then, Stitch appeared in the sky with the ripped tent in her mouth. She swooped down, landed, and dropped the tent on the ground. "The penguins were happy to give their ripped tent to us, especially after I promised to make them a new one later today. They also said they would be glad to come help. They'll be here in a few minutes, after they finish making a leopard sculpture."

"Perfect," Clara said. She raised her

eyebrows and looked at Stitch. "How would you like a sewing challenge?"

Stitch reared up and whinnied. "I would love nothing more than a sewing challenge!" she said. "Especially if it will mean we can go ice-sliding."

"Would you be willing to use this ripped tent fabric to sew four snowsuits for the glow leopards?"

Stitch widened her eyes. "I have never sewn a snowsuit. And I've never sewn clothes for leopards. I can't wait!"

"Super," Clara said, picking up the tent. "Let's go check with the glow leopards about my plan."

Stitch, Snow, and Clara walked together to the center of the puddle, where the glow leopards were floating on their backs in the water with their legs sticking straight up. "Glenda, Gladys, Gilbert, and Gordon, I'd like to introduce you to Princess Snow and Princess Stitch," Clara said.

The glow leopards stood up and smiled eagerly. "Thank you so much for inviting us!" Gladys said. "Is it time to go ice-sliding yet?"

"Almost," Clara said. "Is there any chance you'd be willing to wear snowsuits while we go ice-sliding?"

"Absolutely!" Gordon said.

"I've always wanted to wear a snowsuit," Gilbert said.

"Me too," Gladys said. "The opportunity

to wear a snow suit honestly doesn't come up much."

"I'm just hoping my snowsuit will be purple," Glenda said. "I get a little tired of always being red."

Stitch laughed. "Four purple glow-leopard snowsuits coming up," she said. The scissors, needle, and thread design on her tiara sparkled. A giant tape measure appeared in the air. It spun around and then glided over to Gladys. In a flash, it measured her legs, body, head, and tail. Then, it measured Glenda, Gilbert, and Gordon. "Looks like all the glow leopards are exactly the same size," Stitch said. "That makes this easier."

Her tiara sparkled some more, and a giant pair of gold scissors appeared. The ripped tent floated out of Clara's hands, unfolded, and hovered in the air. In a gold blur, the scissors cut the tent into pieces. Then, in a flash of light, the scissors vanished, and a spool of violet thread and a gold needle appeared. The thread poked itself through the eye of the needle. The needle launched itself into a frenzy of sewing. After only a few seconds, four leopard-shaped snowsuits hung in the air. Each one had a zipper—made from the zippers on the tent flaps—that started at the tip of the tail and ended at the top of the hood. The remaining pieces of fabric

folded themselves into a neat pile and dropped down onto Stitch's back.

"Those are perfect!" Clara said. She pulled one from the air and held it out for Gladys. "I'll help you put this on."

Gladys stepped into the two front legs and then the two back legs. She pushed her tail through the tail sleeve and her head into the hood. Then, Clara zipped up the snowsuit. Next, Clara grabbed a snowsuit from the air and helped Gilbert put it on. Then she helped Glenda and, finally, Gordon.

As soon as the glow leopards were zipped into their snowsuits, Clara felt cold. She zipped back up her own snowsuit. And then she exhaled with relief. The snowsuits worked: They were holding in the glow leopards' heat!

"I hate to say this," Gladys said, "but it's getting hot in here."

"It really is," Glenda said.

"It feels like August inside my snowsuit," Gilbert said.

"Glow leopards love heat," Gordon said. "But I wouldn't mind being just a tiny bit cooler."

"I know exactly what to do," Clara said. "Come this way with me!"

Clara led the snow leopards, Stitch, and Snow over to the box of balloons. She realized that none of the ice packs in her snowsuit were still frozen. And she figured the glow leopards needed them more than she did. She unzipped her own snowsuit and fished out all the ice packs from her freezer and added them in the box. "Snow," she said, "Could you use your magic to freeze all these balloons and ice packs?"

"Sure," Snow said, looking a little confused. The snowflake design on her tiara sparkled.

A comet of glittery white light swirled around the box. And then the balloons and ice packs froze solid.

Clara skipped over to Glenda, unzipped her snowsuit, and dropped in several frozen balloons. Then she zipped it back up. "Amazing!" Glenda said. "Now I'm the perfect temperature."

"I'm so glad," Clara said, remembering

with a smile that Miranda had said exactly the same thing.

Clara unzipped Gladys's, Gilbert's, and Gordon's snowsuits and dropped in the rest of the frozen balloons and the ice packs. Then she zipped them all back up.

The glow leopards grinned. They roared with joy as they leaped in excited circles

around Clara, Stitch, and Snow. They rolled on the ground. They did somersaults. And then they sat in a row and looked eagerly at Clara.

"Now can we go ice-sliding?" Gladys asked.

"Please?" Gordon, Gilbert, and Glenda said.

Clara nodded and smiled at the glow leopards. "We can go ice-sliding as soon as we make a new slide."

Chapter Five

Clara heard a chirping noise in the distance. She turned and saw a parade of red sleds gliding toward them. At least ten purple penguins were on each sled. The sleds stopped by the snowflake archway, and the entire flock of penguins waddled over to Clara, Snow, Stitch, and the glow leopards.

"Hello again!" Petra said.

"We heard you needed us," Priscilla said.

"How can we help?" Penelope asked.

All the penguins in the flock looked expectantly at Clara.

"How would you like a new art project?" Clara asked.

The penguins began jumping, chirping, flapping their wings, and calling out, "A new art project! A new art project! A new art project!"

Clara giggled. The penguins got just as excited as she did about new art projects.

"If you had a very big chunk of snow and ice, do you think you could carve a massive slide?"

"Yes! Yes! Yes!" the penguins chirped, jumping up and down.

"Would you like just one slide?" Petra asked.

"Or a few different options?" Penelope suggested.

Clara looked at Snow. "What do you think?" she asked.

"The old one had just one slide," Snow said. She cocked her head, and her face brightened. "But I'm realizing that now we have an opportunity to make the ice slide even better. How about if there are a few different slides to choose from?"

"You got it!" Priscilla said. "But how are you going to get us the snow and ice? We're only able to make smaller blocks of ice appear."

Clara looked at Snow. "Could you use your magic to make a big heap of snow and ice?"

Snow grinned. "I know just what to do," she said. Her tiara sparkled, and a giant white cloud appeared over the puddle. The cloud flashed bolts of white lightning. And then a blizzard of snow, hail, and freezing rain formed under it. Clara watched in amazement as the winter storm created an ever-growing mound of ice and snow. After several minutes, the cloud disappeared. And rising from the ground was a mountain of ice and snow as big as Clara's family's house!

The penguins' eyes widened. They jumped and chirped with excitement. And then they waddled as fast as they could over to the mountain. "Don't forget to sculpt a staircase into the side of it for those of us who can't fly!" Clara called out.

"Good idea!" Petra called back.

In a matter of seconds, all the purple penguins were pecking, chiseling, slicing, and molding the snow and ice. In under three minutes, the penguins had finished sculpting a staircase, a platform with a railing, and four different slides: two twisty ones with tunnels and two steep ones without tunnels that went straight down.

"We're finished!" Petra exclaimed.

"What do you think?" Penelope asked.

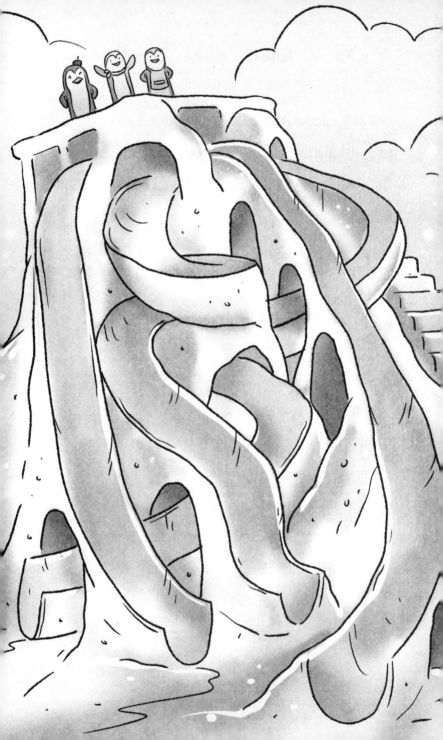

Clara, Snow, and Stitch looked at each other and smiled excitedly.

"It's perfect," Snow said. "Thank you so much."

"It looks incredible," Stitch said to the penguins. "Would you like to join us for ice-sliding?"

"Yes! Yes! Yes!" the penguins cheered.

Just then, six sleds glided up to the archway. On each one rode a pegasus princess. Mist, Aqua, Flip, Star, and Rosie were smiling with excitement. Lucinda grinned as she sat on Star's back. But Clara saw that Dash had a sad, worried look on her face.

Chapter Six

"**W**ow!" Mist said, looking at the ice slides.

"I didn't know you had gotten new slides," Aqua said. "What a great surprise!"

"I can't wait to try them," Star said.

Lucinda flew up into the air and purred.

Flip and Rosie looked at the glow leopards and furrowed their brows. "Are those the snow leopards? Why are they wearing funny outfits and red face paint?" Flip whispered to Clara.

Clara smiled and shook her head. "It turns out the *glow* leopards are joining us today," she whispered back. Then, in a loud voice, she said, "Gladys, Glenda, Gilbert, and Gordon, allow me to introduce you to Princess Mist, Princess Aqua, Princess Flip, Princess Star, Princess Rosie, Princess Dash, and Lucinda."

The pegasus princesses, Lucinda, and the glow leopards smiled and said hello to each other.

"Shall we start ice-sliding?" Snow asked, looking eagerly at the giant ice slides.

"We need to do one thing first," Clara

said. She skipped over to Stitch and whispered her idea in Stitch's ear. Stitch nodded. Clara turned to Dash. "Would you like to try wearing a snowsuit, too? That way you won't feel the ice while you're sliding. Snow and I thought you could call it *nice*-sliding, which is short for not-ice-sliding."

Dash looked at Clara's snowsuit and the glow leopards' snowsuits. She took a long deep breath. And then she smiled. "Yes!" she said, pricking up her ears and suddenly looking excited. "Nice-sliding, here I come!

"One pegasus snowsuit coming up!" Stitch said. Her tiara sparkled. The gold tape measure appeared in the air and flew along Dash's legs, body, and wings. Next, the pile of tent fabric floated up from Stitch's back, and the magic scissors appeared. In a blur of gold, the scissors cut the material into pieces. The needle appeared and sewed the pieces together with violet thread. Before Clara could count to twenty, she was holding a pegasus snowsuit. She held it up to Dash. "I'll help you put this on," she said.

She held it out, and Dash stepped into the four legs. Clara pulled the snowsuit up over the rest of Dash, including her wings, and zipped it up. Dash's eyes widened and a grin spread across her face. "I love wearing this!" she said. "Suddenly, I don't feel the cold air at all!" Dash galloped over to a patch of snow and flopped down into it.

She rolled over on one side and then the other. She flipped onto her legs and galloped back to Clara, her sisters, Lucinda, the glow leopards, and the penguins. "It works!" she called out. "I can't feel the coldness or the slipperiness of the ice through the suit. I can go nice-sliding!"

"Fantastic!" Snow said. "Let's go!" She reared up, whinnied, and galloped toward the ice slides. She looked at the staircase, paused, stretched out her wings and flew to the top. The other seven pegasus princesses all beat their wings and soared up to the platform. Lucinda fluttered right behind them. Clara smiled when she saw that Stitch had designed the snowsuit so Dash could still fly while wearing it.

The glow leopards bounded up the staircase. The penguins waddled behind them. And Clara climbed up last. At the top, Mist, Aqua, Flip, Star, Rosie, Snow, Stitch, and Dash flopped onto the slides and whinnied with joy as they slid down them. Lucinda dived down a steep slide, purring loudly. The glow leopards slid down next, roaring with delight. The penguins plunged down the slides headfirst, happily chirping. And then it was Clara's turn. She decided to first try a twisty tunnel slide. She stepped up to the top of it, sat down on the ice, and pushed herself forward. She slid faster than she had ever slid down a slide before. At the bottom, she shot out of the tunnel and landed in a mound of snow. She laughed, stood up, and ran back to the staircase.

"Let's go down one of the steep slides together," Snow said, galloping alongside Clara.

"Great idea," Clara said.

Snow kneeled next to Clara. "Get on my

back, and we'll fly to the top together," she said. Clara climbed onto Snow. The pegasus soared up into the sky, flew in a loop above the slides, and landed on the platform. Snow kneeled, and Clara got off her back.

"How about that slide?" Snow suggested, glancing at the steepest one. Gladys, Gordon, and five penguins were already shooting down it.

"I'm ready!" Clara said.

She and Snow stepped to the top of the slide. "One. Two. Three. Jump!" Snow said.

She and Clara jumped forward onto the slide. They barreled down it, side-by-side, laughing together the whole time.

"That was amazing!" Snow said when they landed at the bottom.

"I love ice-sliding!" Clara said.

Clara slid down the ice slides over and over again. After she had tried the tunnel slides six times each and the steep slides ten times each, she realized that while it had been wonderful to visit the Wing Realm, her hands and her head were cold. She also missed her sister and their snowy mountain game. And she was in the mood for hot chocolate.

Clara turned to Snow and the other pegasus princesses, who were just finishing a round of sliding. "I hate to say this," Clara said, "but I think it's time for me to return to the human world."

"I completely understand," Snow said. "Thank you so much for joining us."

"Thank you for saving ice-sliding," Stitch said.

Snow nodded. "And thank you for thinking of a way to include the glow leopards. Now we've made four new friends."

"And thank you for suggesting Stitch make me a snowsuit," Dash said. "I thought I was going to have a cold, miserable afternoon, and now I'm having a great time."

Lucinda purred and rubbed against Clara's legs.

"I'm so glad I could help," Clara said. "Thank you for including me."

"We'll invite you back to the Wing Realm soon," Snow said with a wink.

"Goodbye!" Mist, Aqua, and Rosie said.

"Thanks for joining us," Stitch said.

"It was great to see you!" Dash said.

Flip smiled warmly and swished her tail.

The glow leopards smiled and waved their paws.

Clara pulled the silver feather from her snowsuit pocket. She held it up and said, "Take me home, please!"

Clara smiled as the feather lifted her up in the air, higher and higher. She began to spin, and everything went pitch black. After a few seconds, she found herself sitting on the forest floor under the giant pine tree. The sun shone down at her. And she noticed she was already getting too hot. But then she felt something cold brushing against her hand. She looked down. There next to her was a mesh bag full of purple, penguin-shaped ice packs, all frozen solid. Clara giggled. She unzipped her snowsuit and dropped the cold penguins inside it. Laughing, she rolled and somersaulted on the pine straw to move the penguins around in her suit. And then, when she was the perfect temperature, she scooped up some pine needles to use for snow leopard beds and ran home to her sister.

Don't miss our other new high-flying adventure!

Turn the page for a sneak peek...

Clara raced along the hallway, down the stairs, through the living room, and across the kitchen. She burst out the back door and hopped across the slate stones that led to the woods surrounding her house. As she stepped into the forest, she realized she hadn't closed the back door. In fact, she hadn't even heard the outer screen door latch shut. She knew she really ought to go back and close both doors. But she was so excited to visit the Wing Realm that, instead of turning around, Clara kept running.

She leaped over a creek where she and her sister liked to make potions. She barreled down a hill, pulled the feather from her pocket, and skipped into a clearing with a large pine tree. A second later, glittery light swirled. And then there appeared a green velvet armchair with silver wings on its back. The armchair jumped up and down. It leaped over to Clara, spun around on one leg, and nudged her. Clara laughed and patted the top of the chair. "It's good to see you, too," Clara said.

She was about to sit down on the chair when she felt something pressing against her calves. Clara looked behind her. No Name Yet was jumping up and pushing her paws against the backs of Clara's legs. The puppy wagged her tail and panted. "Did you escape from the house and follow me here?" Clara asked, laughing and picking up No Name Yet.

Clara paused and considered what to do. One option was to run back to her house and put No Name Yet inside. But that would leave the puppy feeling sad and lonely. And it would delay Clara's visit to the Wing Realm. Another option, Clara realized with a burst of excitement, was to bring the puppy with her. Clara kissed

No Name Yet's head and said, "Get ready to meet to meet the pegasus princesses!"

Holding No Name Yet a little tighter in her arms, Clara sat down on the armchair. She grabbed No Name Yet's collar as the chair jumped up and landed on top of the large pine tree. For a moment the tree and the chair swayed back and forth. The puppy yipped with excitement. Then the chair soared upward, skidded across the roof of Clara's house, and launched up into the sky. The chair flew higher and higher. It began to spin, faster and faster. Everything went pitch black. And then, in a few seconds, the chair landed with a clatter on a tile floor.

Clara opened her eyes. She knew exactly where she was: the front hall of Feather Palace. The black floor shimmered under the light of the chandeliers. On the walls, painted magenta, hung portraits of all eight pegasus princesses and their silver pet cat Lucinda. Pegasus statues reared up with outstretched wings from marble pedestals. Pegasus fountains spouted rainbow water. The pegasus princesses' eight thrones formed a horseshoe in the center of the room. Pushed up against Rosie's pink throne was Lucinda's silver sofa, with its back shaped like a cat head. In the middle of the cushion, Lucinda lay curled in a ball, fast asleep. Her head rested on the star-shaped pillow Clara had given Lucinda for her birthday.

Clara heard a voice call out behind her, "Let's practice one more time. We've almost got it." With No Name Yet still in her arms, Clara stood up and turned around. All eight pegasus princesses stood in a tight circle with their eyes closed. Rosie counted, "A one and a two and a one two three four." The pegasus princesses nodded their heads to the beat as they danced, tapping and sliding their front and back hooves against the tiles in intricate rhythms. As Clara watched, she found herself quietly tapping her flip-flops against the floor and wishing she could join in. No Name Yet seemed to feel the same way. The puppy wiggled and squirmed in Clara's arms. Clara hugged her more tightly and whispered, "Hold on just a minute. You'll be able to get down soon."

When the pegasus princesses finished tapping and sliding, Rosie said, "That time was perfect. Thank you so much for all your hard work and practice. I'm thrilled to say we're ready for the concert."

Emily Bliss, also the author of the Unicorn Princesses series, lives with her winged cat in a house surrounded by woods. From her living room window, she can see silver feathers and green flying armchairs. Like Clara Griffin, she knows pegasuses are real.

Sydney Hanson was raised in Minnesota alongside numerous pets and brothers. She is the illustrator of the Unicorn Princesses series and the picture books *Next to You*, *Escargot*, and *A Book for Escargot*, among many others. Sydney lives in Los Angeles.

www.sydwiki.tumblr.com